Little Red Riding Hood

Illustrations by J. L. MACIAS S.   Retold by JANE CARRUTH

Once upon a time there was a pretty little girl who lived with her Mummy and Daddy close to a big wood. Everybody called her Red Riding Hood because she always wore a red cape and hood.

On the far side of the big wood lived Red Riding Hood's grandmother and, one day, the little girl set out to visit her.

Little Red Riding Hood loved her grandmother and she was glad her Mummy had filled her basket with honey and cakes to take to her. Her Mummy had told her to go all the way around the wood because of the big bad wolf who lived there. But it was such a sunny day that Red Riding Hood forgot all about the wolf.

She went into the wood and, oh dear, quite soon she met that big bad wolf. "Good morning to you," said the wolf, in a soft, kind voice. "Where are you going?"

"To see my grandmother," said Red Riding Hood. "I'm taking her some honey and cakes because she isn't very well today."

The big bad wolf was very cunning. He pretended to be sad that Red Riding Hood's grandmother was not very well. And he soon found out just where she lived. "You gather some flowers to take to her," he said at last. "I must be off!"

Goodness, how fast that big bad wolf ran through the woods! He did not draw breath until he had found the grandmother's cottage and was knocking at the door. "It's your own Red Riding Hood," he called gently. "Unbolt the door and let me in."

No sooner was the wolf inside than he gobbled up the old lady. Then he wrapped her shawl around his shoulders, put on her pink nightcap and balanced her spectacles on his nose. "Now I'll wait for Red Riding Hood," he thought, as he jumped into bed.

He did not have long to wait. He had only time to pull the cover right up to his face before Red Riding Hood arrived.
"How are you?" she asked, going up to the bed. "I've brought you some pretty flowers and a basket full of good things."

Then Red Riding Hood looked at her grandmother more closely, as the wolf croaked, "Come and give your Granny a kiss, child!"

"But Grandmama, what big ears you have got!"

"All the better to hear you with," said the wolf.

"And, oh Grandmama, what big eyes you have got."

"All the better to see you with," said the wolf.

"And Grandmama, what big teeth you have got!"

"All the better to eat you with," snarled the big bad wolf, and he sprang out of bed.

Poor little Red Riding Hood was so frightened that she dropped her basket and tried to escape. But the wolf caught her and gobbled her up.

Then he felt so heavy with the old lady and Red Riding Hood inside him that he climbed back into bed and fell asleep.

Now, two farm workers had seen the big bad wolf enter the old lady's cottage. "We had better go and find out if she is safe," they said to each other. Imagine their horror when they saw the wolf in bed and the room turned upside down. "The wolf has gobbled up the old lady for sure," said one.

"And the little girl," said the other. "We had better cut him open as fast as we can."

So the two brave men went into the cottage and they cut open the wolf, who was sleeping so heavily that he did not wake up, which was just as well, for out of his big stomach hopped the old lady and after her came little Red Riding Hood!

And while Red Riding Hood and her grandmother ran outside to hide in the woods, the two farm workers filled the wolf's stomach with heavy stones and then sewed it up.

When the big bad wolf did wake up he felt so heavy and thirsty that he staggered out of the cottage and made his way to the pond for a drink. But the stones moved inside his stomach. He over-balanced and fell into the water and soon drowned.

When the old lady heard the wolf was dead, she took Red Riding Hood back to the cottage. She hugged and kissed the little girl and said that all the excitement had made her feel much better. Then they tidied up the room and had cakes and honey for tea. So, after all, it was a happy day for them both.

Published in United States and simultaneously in Canada by Joshua Morris,
431 Post Road East, Westport, CT 0
Printed in Bel